Some Sleep Standing Up

Susan Stockdale

SIMON & SCHUSTER BOOKS FOR YOUNG READERS

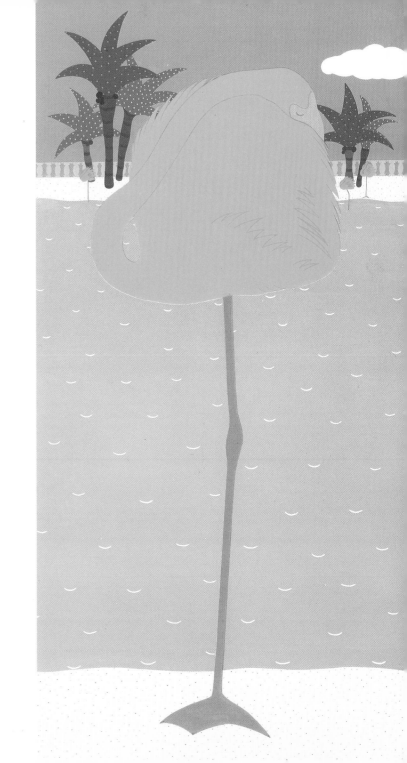

SIMON & SCHUSTER BOOKS FOR YOUNG READERS

An imprint of Simon & Schuster Children's Publishing Division

1230 Avenue of the Americas, New York, New York 10020

Copyright © 1996 by Susan Stockdale

All rights reserved including the right of reproduction in whole or in part in any form.

SIMON & SCHUSTER BOOKS FOR YOUNG READERS is a trademark of Simon & Schuster.

Book design by Paul Zakris. The text of this book is set in 28-point Bodega Sans Black Oldstyle.

The illustrations are rendered in acrylic

Manufactured in the United States of America

First Edition

10 9 8 7 6 5 4 3 2 1

Library of Congress Cataloging-in-Publication Data

Stockdale, Susan R.

Some Sleep Standing Up / Susan Stockdale.

p. cm.

Summary: Illustrates numerous different ways in which animals sleep

such as sprawling in a heap, dreaming in a tree, and dozing on one leg.

1. Sleep behavior in animals—Juvenile literature.   [1. Animals—Sleep behavior.

2. Sleep.   3. Animals—Habits and behavior.]   I. Title.

QL755.3.S76   1996   591.51—dc20   95-35924   CIP   AC

ISBN 0-689-80509-8

for Chelsea and Justin,
who sleep lying down.

Animals sleep in all kinds of ways.

Some rest with eyes open,

some relax with them closed.

Some snore way up high,

some snooze way down low.

Some dream in trees,

some prefer leaves.

Some sprawl in a heap,

some spread out in a hive.

Some sleep standing up,

some like to lie down.

Some doze on one leg,

some drowse on two.

Some nap right side up,

some nod upside down.

Some slumber by night,

some slumber by day.

But they all sleep just right
in their own special way.

Like you.